When you were a baby I sat very
still to hold you. I could see
the veins through your skin like
a map to inside you. I stopped
breathing so you wouldn't. . . .

You were just a boy on a bed in
a room, like a kaleidoscope is a
tube full of bits of broken glass.
But the way I saw you was pieces
refracting the light,shifting into
an infinite universe of flowers
and rainbows and insects and
planets, magical dividing cells,
pictures no one else knew. . . .

Your whole life you can be
told something is wrong and so
you believe it.

Wasteland

FRANCESCA LIA BLOCK

JOANNA COTLER BOOKS

An Imprint of HarperCollins*Publishers*

Pages 126–128: "Marina" from *Collected Poems 1909–1962* by T.S. Eliot, copyright 1936 by
Harcourt, Inc., copyright © 1964, 1963 by T.S. Eliot, reprinted by permission of the publisher.

Pages 24, 51, 61, 62: Selections from "The Waste Land" from *Collected Poems 1909–1962*
by T.S. Eliot, copyright 1936 by Harcourt, Inc., copyright © 1964, 1963 by T.S. Eliot.

Printed in the United States of America. For information address HarperCollins
Children's Books, a division of HarperCollins Publishers,
1350 Avenue of the Americas, New York, NY 10019.
www.harpercollins.com

Library of Congress Cataloging-in-Publication Data
Block, Francesca Lia.
 Wasteland / by Francesca Lia Block.— 1st ed.
  p.   cm.
 Summary: A brother and sister must deal with terrible consequences when their love for
each other stretches past acceptable boundaries.
 ISBN 0-06-028644-X — ISBN 0-06-028645-8 (lib. bdg.) — ISBN 0-06-440839-6 (pbk.)
 [1. Brothers and sisters—Fiction. 2. Incest—Fiction. 3. Los Angeles (Calif.)—Fiction.] I. Title.
PZ7. B61945Was 2003   2002155593
[Fic]—dc21

Typography by Alicia Mikles

First paperback edition, 2004

Thank you Joanna Cotler, Lydia Wills,
Tracey Porter, and Suza Scalora

You

*W*E KEEP BURNING *in the brown smog pit. The girls swarm in their black moth dresses. Their scalps are shaved like concentration camp ladies. Rats click my head. Everything broken.*

When you were a baby I sat very still to hold you. I could see the veins through your skin like a map to inside you. How could skin be that thin? I was so afraid you might drop and break. I stopped breathing so you wouldn't.

When you were crying I got out of bed and went into your room. You were thrashing around behind the bars of the crib, your face twisted and red, like, how could they be doing this to me? I didn't understand why Mom hadn't come to you.

You turned your head to look at me. Your eyes looked so big in your face, so mysterious—wide and flickering like a butterfly-wing mask. When you saw me the wails turned to sobs, and then just quieter heaves of your body. I held out my finger through the bars.

Then you reached out and curled your fingers around mine, so tight. I knew you recognized me. That was the first time I knew I had a heart inside my body.

You still cry too easily, but without your tears, at least, everything would burn. You are Spring in your jeans, in the laughing leaves. I think pearls melted over your bones.

I thought sacrifice might mean something. The wounds throb even though they're not real yet. Would you reach inside them to uncover the secret? You try to tell me but your tongue feels severed.

Kaleidoscope

You were just a boy on a bed in a room, like a kaleidoscope is a tube full of bits of broken glass. But the way I saw you was pieces refracting the light, shifting into an infinite universe of flowers and rainbows and insects and planets, magical dividing cells, pictures no one else knew.

I remember. I was going on a date and I came into your room. I wanted you to see me, but I pretended I was coming to see if you had any beers in the ice chest under your bed. I was wearing my shiny leotard and my wraparound skirt, my cork sandals and Jontue perfume and Bonne

Bell lip gloss. I had shaved my legs and they were pretty tan already, even though it was May. I knocked and you didn't answer. I thought the music was too loud and you hadn't heard. It was this crazy banging shouting music I'd never heard before. I just opened the door.

You jerked up and looked at me. You were in bed with the sheet over you and the room smelled close. I smelled your pot and beer and your smell—salty, warm, baked. I read in a magazine that women aren't supposed to be attracted to the smells of their fathers and brothers.

You sat up and your eyes were blank and hard—mad. You yelled, What are you doing? Don't you knock anymore!

I backed up and your eyes turned sad, then kind. You said, I'm sorry, you. Hang on, and I turned and pretended to look at some albums while you got up. You were buttoning your black jeans when I turned around. But you didn't have a shirt on. You looked pale—usually you were tan by spring, too, darker than me—but your skin was white and smooth like marble. I could see every segment of muscle in your stomach; your arms looked stronger, too. There were some weights on the floor. I apologized and you sat on the bed and asked me what I wanted. You never asked me that when I came to you. We just accepted the pull that brought us into the same spaces as often as possible. I mumbled something about the beer. I wanted you to like my outfit, I wanted your praise because without it I felt like I was going to fade into nothing. This little shiny leotard and rayon jersey wrap skirt would walk out all alone on platform sandals to meet my date.

You said, Where are you going? You sounded like a dad and it scared me. I said dancing. You asked where and I said, Kaleidoscope. You rolled your eyes. Why that disco shit? You never spoke to me like that. I could feel my face getting hot. I hoped my tan and the Indian Earth makeup on my cheeks and eyelids would hide it. I smelled my perfume and it was way too sweet; I wanted to smell like you. You saw me getting upset and you said you were sorry again. You asked if I was going on a date, I looked pretty. I said kind of. Michelle and I were meeting some boys. You asked who was driving. I said Michelle. You said you didn't want us drinking. You asked if you could drive. I said no. I didn't want you to see me with Brent Fisher. I was afraid you'd tease me about him forever. You shrugged. You said, Whatever, have fun, and you lay back on your bed and closed your eyes.

I came home at about 2:30. My leotard was sopping wet. I had sweated off all my lotion and perfume and deodorant and I kept sniffing my armpits on my way upstairs, touching with one fingertip and sniffing. I wondered if you could smell the beer that Brent Fisher and Billy Ellis got for us. I was chewing some Bubble Yum to try to hide it. The sugar coated my mouth but bitter, the sweet was all gone, like I'd sipped perfume.

I knocked and you answered. I couldn't believe it when I saw you . Your head was shaved. I thought you looked so naked and different, vulnerable and ugly and beautiful. If I hadn't been drunk I might have been able to pretend I was cool but I was drunk and you saw me staring and shrugged and turned around and went back in. I followed you because you didn't close the door. You sat back on the floor and ignored me. I just stood there looking at the shape of your head that I hadn't seen since you were a little boy and Mom made you get a crew cut. Your head was symmetrical and proud like a Roman statue's—like that replica of David that Mom had in the den—but your ears stuck out and the bone at the nape of your neck looked knobby. I wanted to touch your scalp. You used to look like Jim Morrison. I asked about your head. You said it was punkrock (you said it like one word) and I probably didn't know what that was. I said I knew, too, I did so know. I sounded like a baby. You said you were sorry but disco sucked and I needed to be educated. I rolled my eyes but I wanted you to go on. You said it was a movement from the U.K., very radical, it was about breaking rules and making your own sounds. You said maybe I should cut my hair. You had never said anything like that. I wanted to cry. I said I was going to bed.

I went to my room and unpeeled. My wet clothes lay in a heap. My shoes looked precarious and stupid. I wondered if I would ever be brave enough to wear punk shoes, although I wasn't sure what that was for girls. As I lay on my waterbed I touched my head. It felt small and bumpy. The waves rippled under me and I pretended I was on a houseboat, as far away from the Valley as I could get without leaving you for another ocean.

Jealous

Mom said, Lex, you look so nice today, honey, smoothing your hair, pushing it out of your eyes, and you said, Marina picked this lame shirt out, and you winked at me. She said, We've got to do something about all this hair, though. Or she said, How was school today, Lex? and you said, It sucked. Marina, did your day suck as much as mine? Once, in front of you, she told me I had reached that age when I wasn't a sweet-smelling little girl anymore and we needed to get me some Secret. Later you said, She's just jealous. I asked what you meant but you wouldn't answer.

Burn

MY MIND IS LIKE THE VALLEY—this vast barren waste. Car lots. Malls. Tract homes. I know there are other worlds beyond it—of canyons full of coyote and monarch butterflies, squirrels, bunnies, purple and yellow wildflowers, of magical boulevards lined with palatial movie theaters and movie-star haunted mansions, of parks and palms and palisades, especially, especially of the ocean, where it all ends and everything begins. I know the rest is out there but from where I sit in my head it's like being on the bottom of a hot sunken pit—you can't see anything else around you no matter how hard you try.

Before you could drive and got the wagon we took the bus to the beach. It picked us up on Ventura Boulevard and went over Sepulveda, through Westwood and all the way to Santa Monica. We knew the water wasn't too clean there, there were reports that people got sick from swimming in the bay but we didn't care. We kicked off our flip-flops, ran across the sand that burned our soles, and fell onto our beach towels. You read Kerouac and I brought *Seventeen*, *Mademoiselle*, *Glamour*, and *Vogue*. I lay in a daze, blinking at the twinkles of white light on the blue waves, feeling the beautiful heat deep in my hair, salt water evaporating from my skin, leaving it smoother against my bones. The sand scratched under my bikini and I'd peek to see the contrast between the pale skin there and the rosebrown color of my belly, almost black where the hipbones poked up. We'd swim; we'd plunge into the salty stingy lunge of waves. We'd come out and you'd toss your head and drip drops from your hair on me. We'd stop for rocky road ice cream in Westwood on the way home and I picked out the nuts and gave them to you, you plucked marshmallows for me. I'd sleep next to you on the bus. Once my head slipped onto your shoulder while I was half asleep. I waited. You didn't try to wake me up.

Once I lay in the sun so long, slicked with baby oil, that I blistered on my chin and chest. Shiny clear bubbles over the red. Pale clear liquid seeping out. You put ointment on it and ice and said to be careful. You could tan so easily—I wondered if our dad was pale like I am. Even Mom didn't get as dark as you, though. Sometimes I wanted to peel away all of my skin and find a different me underneath.

Mermaid

YOU ASKED IF I BELIEVED in reincarnation. You doodled on a napkin, carnation carnivore carnal. I said I wasn't sure. You said if you died you'd come back as an animal—a dog. You'd always wanted a dog but Mom said we couldn't have one in the house, it would ruin the carpeting and the furniture and she said she'd end up having to pick up its shits while we were out partying. That second part wouldn't have been true—we would have been good dog parents, especially you. You always fed strays and bent down to talk to the dogs you met on the street, looking straight into their eyes as if they were old friends. (Maybe they are, you said. From another life.) You liked to go to the pound and look at them. You tried to send them messages of comfort. I couldn't go because I started crying the one time I tried. All those eyes and the barks like sobs. You said that if you came back as a dog you'd find me and I could be your owner. I thought it was weird you were talking about that but you liked to talk about death. You said our society needed to talk more about it and not be so uptight—death was just another phase and maybe a better one. The beginning of something, right? You wondered if we knew each other before. If you were my baby, if you were my father. We weren't sister and brother, you said. We were something else.

You asked me who I thought I was before. I said maybe I was a fish because I love water and you said, you thought a mermaid, maybe.

If you were a mermaid, you said, If you were a mermaid, I was the sea.

Blood

I REMEMBER. I was thirteen. You came to me in math class. Everyone had left and I was still sitting there, pretending to do homework. I had asked Michelle to go and get you. I could have told her, I guess, but I didn't. I wanted you. I was scared and you were always who I went to when I was scared.

I was practically stuck to my seat. The wetness pooling underneath me. I looked up at you. You had come running. There was sweat on your face, your eyes all pupil. Hey, you, you said, down on your knees looking at me. Hey you what is it you scared me you okay?

I looked down at my lap and you knew what it was. You took off your sweatshirt and put it around me. You tied it on my hips. You helped me up. My body sticky and hot. The cramps were roiling, tight pain. You held me against you for a second. I could feel your heart beating through your pilling green-and-white-striped gym shirt. I wanted to sink down again into you. If I were you I would be tall and strong and I'd never bleed like this, this shame stain pain of blood every month until I get old. I was old, all of a sudden. I wanted to be a little girl. A little boy.

You walked behind me, like you were protecting me. I was wearing white sailor jeans which I scrubbed and bleached later but ended up having to throw out. Your dark green sweatshirt was the best thing I'd ever worn. You drove me home. You didn't tell Mom. You stole some pads from her bathroom. I was supposed to keep some of my own for when this happened—they had given them to us in Health. But I threw them away. I figured I might be lucky, it might never come. I was wrong. I had to fasten the pad on with this stupid belt with the plastic clips. I hated the bulk of it. You said we'd go get something better at the drug store. You weren't embarrassed. You paid for the tampons.

What did it mean for us? Because everything I did, everything that happened to me, that was what I asked myself—what does this mean for us. It meant I was farther away from you, different. It meant that if we let ourselves, we could get closer than we had ever been. Disappear into each other. You'd bleed and I wouldn't. Then we both would.

You

YOU DIED. You were sitting on the bleachers in P.E. when Ms. Sand told you to go to the principal's office. You were peeling the yellow rubber thing that said N.H.H.S. off of your green gym shorts and chewing your fingernails on the other hand. You could taste the bitter peel of polish. You were staring down through the slats of the bleachers to the gym floor. You were not even forcing tears back down because there weren't any because you were dead.

You, that's me. You called me you and I called you you. That was our name for each other. When you died I did and so it didn't matter.

MARINA RAN. Out of the principal's office before they could stop her.

West ran faster. He caught up with her on Magnolia under the trees with the flesh-thick white flowers. They had both climbed the fence out of the school prison; the skin on her leg was torn, raked on metal spikes. She looked like she was going to fall onto the sidewalk. Her face was red blotches over blanched white and her eyes looked like cracked green glass. The sweat and tears mixing on her face so he couldn't tell which was which. Her chest was heaving with running, with sobbing. A vein in her neck was pulsing like it might burst. He imagined trying to hold her together while rivers of pain hissed out between his fingers onto the hot tarred pavement.

She fought him at first with her ragged peeling fingernails and her fists against his chest. He held on until she weakened, slumped against him, shaking, the way girls did in class, jiggling their knees on their chairs, but this was her whole body paroxysms. She felt so small, like a little girl, like he could lift her in his arms, and he wasn't that much bigger. She kept saying, Lex, Lex, Lex. Wailing. He made sounds because he didn't have a single word for her, comforting sounds he hoped. He wished he was an animal who wasn't expected to use words. He didn't have a single word. Your brother is dead. The person you love more than anyone. He's dead and you're only sixteen. Nothing is okay, it might never be okay. I love you but I know it doesn't matter now and maybe it never will. There is nothing I can say.

Around them it was hot stillness like everything holding its breath. No cars even passed and the usually sizzling leaves hung in silence over them. The heat and the fumes of the Valley were quiet. He closed his eyes and saw the ocean.

See

*THEY ARE ALL OVER THE CITY, these lit-
tle storefronts with pink neon signs that say PSYCHIC.
Crystal balls and pyramids and heads of Nefertiti in
the windows. I don't know how they all manage to
stay in business; maybe they are covers for drug
operations or something. Sometimes the women
watch me through the windows or beckon me from
the doorways. Do they do that to everyone? It's like
they can tell I'm susceptible. I think of prophecies
written on leaves, visions of fire, voices in the
thunder. I want to go to the women, every time. I
want to know what they see. And then part of me
is afraid. That if they say what I know is there it*

will be undeniable, it will be real. That they will see nothing.

Once I went to one. Her place smelled of too sweet smoke and there were fake red roses and a fat cat with a jeweled collar. The candle had an electric flame. I thought, What am I doing here? She looked so bored I thought she might fall asleep. But then she started tapping her fingernails on the tabletop. Rap rap rap. Something was troubling her? I thought, Here it comes. I thought, "Fear death by water. Those are pearls that were his eyes. Look!" *She said, There's someone who loves you too much. Too much. She shook her head and squinted through me. I was caving in, my guts collapsing; part of me felt so relieved. She said, You aren't who you think you are. She said, I can tell you more. It'll be fifty dollars. Do you have it? I can help you, tell you more. Fifty dollars. I got on my bike and rode as fast as I could. What more could she tell me? I already knew. I was Tiresias who had seen the goddess, seen too* much. I was struck blind, impotent. I could see everything. I was the Sibyl hanging upside down. She asked Apollo to live forever. He granted her wish but she got older and older smaller and smaller shriveled finally to nothing.

Kids Who Died

I REMEMBER WHEN Marty Fallbrook died. He was this skinny boy with buckteeth. He was in love with Michelle and she was better to him than a lot of girls would have been. She didn't laugh at him. She told him gently that she couldn't go to the dance with him, that she liked to dance with her friends. She let go of Billy Ellis's hand when she saw Marty in the hall. Marty laughed a lot. He was always laughing at himself. Even at his crush on Michelle. He had a high-pitched laugh that made everyone laugh even more. With me, not at me, he seemed to be saying with his laugh. I'm laughing, too. With me, not at me. He was in love with Michelle, I think, it wasn't just a crush. With her long, shiny, straight hair and her strong athletic legs and her naturally dark skin and her Brooke Shields eyebrows. I knew he was in love with her, in that serious way. I knew that look. It was like you became just this pair of eyes watching and wanting and the rest of you vanishing into nothing. And then he did. He was riding his moped without a helmet and he crashed on Mulholland. You said, It wasn't an accident. I asked how you knew, but I knew too. You said that crush he had on Michelle, that was serious. I said you were wrong, it was an accident. But I knew you were right. I knew Marty Fallbrook drank some beers he'd stolen from his parents and got on his moped without his helmet and went for it on Mulholland, on those crazy winding roads above the valley where people park to watch the lights and fuck. With me, not at me.

WEST WENT TO THE FUNERAL at Forest Lawn Cemetery. It was big rolling green lawns with ugly replicas of Greek and Roman statues everywhere. Pretty fancy, he thought. Not very Lex at all. He figured it was Lex's mother's idea.

Not many people were there. The A.P. English teacher, Mr. Montgomery, with another guy who didn't have the neat little mustache but otherwise looked a lot like him. West figured that was his boyfriend. Lex's cross-country coach, Mr. Jamison, stood in the back. West saw some punk girls he didn't recognize huddling together and sobbing. Marina's mom was wearing a tight black dress. She had a few people with her, including a younger guy in a shiny suit who was holding her arm. West looked around for someone who might be Lex and Marina's father. Marina was wearing a black sweatshirt and black jeans and boots and a pair of sunglasses that looked like the ones Lex used to have. She didn't have any makeup on and her face was pale. She wasn't crying at all. This was what scared him the most. Where had she locked up the things he'd seen her feeling that day when she heard? She wasn't that big a girl to hold all of it—to hold her brother's life and his death inside of her. To hold all his long-limbed raging tidal motion and all the loss of that.

West didn't cry either.

Kids Who Died

YOU REMEMBER THE ONES who die when you're a kid. You remember them because it's so out of control and it reminds you that it's not just old people even though you feel in a million years nothing could happen to you. You could dance on train tracks and jump from moving vehicles and skateboard in the wash during flash flood season. But then something happens like Traci Todd. She had a button nose and a soft lispy voice and twinkly eyes and soft kitteny hair. She was always giving you a piece of gum or sharing her lip gloss which smelled like coconuts. Traci Todd, with a daisy for the i at the end of her name, always seemed to be smiling like a year-book photo of the most popular girl.

Traci was the last one you'd pick—if you were going through a yearbook—to die. You'd think she'd get married really young and drive a Mercedes and live in a cute house and have a couple of babies and maybe go into real estate and have grandchildren and lots of parties and anniversaries and wear lots of cute shoes and aerobicize and go to Hawaii for vacations and receive heaps of flowers. The last thing came true at her funeral, to which everyone came. She'd gotten hit by a car driven by a drunk driver crossing the street while on vacation at a ski resort. We wondered what happened when the car hit her, and then we tried not to think about it in spite of our nightmares, which were like a collective one that didn't seem like it would end. We all cried for a week. Girls bursting into hysterical sobs, collapsing on the track, screaming in math class. Her mom invited all the girls to come over and take one item of clothing if we wanted. I wanted this one fluffy baby blue sweater but I couldn't bring myself to take it. It seemed like a sacred thing, a relic. Afterward I'd see her clothes on other girls—T-shirts with satin hearts quilted on the front, jeans with butterfly appliqués, white cotton sundresses embroidered with baby flowers, and pink-and-lavender-striped spandex tops. I don't think anybody forgot who they belonged to once. When I'd see her mom at the store I couldn't look at her. Finally I made myself say hi and she seemed so happy—I think most people just stopped talking to her after that. Like, what can you say? Now I know. Nothing. There is nothing to say. But Traci Todd. You came into my room the night after her funeral. You said you were there, in the back, you didn't want to have to deal with all my friends. I said I was looking for you. I wished I'd seen you. You said it wasn't fair. Over and over again you kept saying that. You said, There are so many kids that want to die. She's probably the one that wanted to live the most. I thought, no, I want to live as much as she did. But only if . . . and then I realized how much it sucked for me to think that. Think about myself like that, complain. I was here and I could go dancing and sweat all night and eat donuts and go roller-skating and take bubble baths and grow up. I had you. Right there with me. I had you living in my life and I was alive.

MARINA WAS OUT OF SCHOOL for a week.
West went by her house a few times but no one
answered. Once her mom came to the door and
said Marina didn't want to see anybody. Without
her sunglasses the mom looked a lot older. She
had big green eyes like Marina but he couldn't
see Lex in her at all. She was manicured and
wearing expensive jeans. She worked out, you
could tell. Her hair was dyed blond. There were
big black-and-white blowup photos of her and
Marina and Lex on the wall of the living room.
West remembered from the times he'd gone over
there. Lex and Marina hated the pictures, they

embarrassed them. Their mother was an interior decorator and it was her thing and they couldn't do anything about it. It was a party, when he'd been there. The mom was out and she'd said it was okay and there were kids everywhere raiding the booze cabinet and lying around on the white couches. Marina had on a T-shirt that laced up the front and pale yellow jeans and her hair was all tousled. She smelled like vanilla and flowers and bubble gum and beer. Lex was drinking too much and there were lots of tossing, shiny, stretchy, glossy girls around him but he didn't seem to care about them. He and West went into the back bushes and shared a bong load. The house was in the canyon overlooking the valley. The pool was jewel blue and hazed in mist. Oleanders rustled around them, prickly and poisonous. Heat lay over the Valley, glazing the red, green, gold, white lights. The bong gurgled. Lex handed it to West. He looked out across the lights. He said, Sometimes I don't think she's real. West didn't say anything. He knew who Lex was talking about. He wasn't shocked. He understood so well and maybe that was what scared him.

But now, standing at the front door of the house with its glittering, silver-embedded white walls, its slit windows, its little palm trees, its fake gold dome, he was waiting to see Marina and she was locked up like a princess in a fairy tale and he felt like he could never find her.

Even when she came back to school he felt that way. He watched her slouching around. She was wearing one of Lex's sweatshirts—a green one. She looked like she'd lost some weight, or maybe it was just the big clothes. She didn't have any lip gloss on or perfume and she was pale. He said hi in the hallway and she just looked at him. He'd never seen anyone die before but he thought that she was dying.

Goodbye Yellow Brick Road

IT WAS NEW YEAR'S EVE. We went over to Michelle's with three bottles of André champagne and two straws. Each of us had a bottle and Michelle and I had straws. We sat on lawn chairs on Michelle's roof and listened to all our albums. We listened to *Goodbye Yellow Brick Road* over and over again. We studied the pictures and looked for dirty lyrics. Your favorite song on that album was "Candle in the Wind." I thought you looked like you were crying but it might have been the champagne and the gold lights. I sipped my champagne fast, fizzing up my nose. I got up to dance by myself when the fireworks from the park started. We could see them from the roof. You liked the cherry bombs but I didn't because they were just loud explosions. I liked the big cascades of fiery flowers. Michelle and I gasped and oohed and ahhed. You gulped down the rest of your champagne and belched and we laughed. You stood at the edge of the roof and spread your arms out like a bird. I felt like I was at the beginning of something, like my life was going to happen. The air was cool on my skin that smelled of chlorine and Bain de Soleil. The champagne made me fizz inside. I rubbed my arms, I had goose bumps. I saw you look over at me from the edge of the roof. I knew you wanted to give me your sweatshirt but then you looked over at Michelle and you didn't. It was okay. I felt the warmth of fleece and your body heat against my skin anyway. I cuddled up with Michelle on the chaise and watched you lit up in a burning flash. The sky exploded inside of me. We were so happy to the soundtrack of the organs on "Funeral for a Friend."

WEST CAME UP TO MARINA when she was eating an apple out of a brown paper bag in the quad. Her hair looked like she hadn't washed it for about a week. Blond squiggles fell over her eyes. She had a few red marks on her face and her fingernails were bitten, flecked with chewed red polish. Her lips were just as full as always, he saw. He tried to remember how she looked when she smiled—the perfect flash of it, like a movie star, like she was saying she loved you with her smile. It was hard to imagine it now.

West sat next to her. He remembered the first time he saw her. She was dressed like a surfer

boy in a woven Mexican shirt, cords, Vans sneak-
ers, and puka shells. They were in seventh grade.
Her hair was long then, almost to her waist. She
walked like a boy. She smelled of baby powder.
He saw her with Lex. They were walking
together and laughing and he thought that must
be her boyfriend. Lex wore shells, too. His long
curly hair fell over a lean, chiseled face. He was
slightly bowlegged and wore a faded orange Val
Surf T-shirt.

When West found out Lex was Marina's
brother he went up to him and asked him where
he surfed. Lex said Zuma. West said him, too.
Lex said, Hey, us Vals have to stick together.
West said maybe they'd catch a few waves some
time. He imagined Marina sitting on the sand
watching them.

But he started to love Lex, too, that was the
thing. Lex surfed wicked, like the devil. He wasn't
afraid of anything, seemed like. He grinned at
West as the waves came up toward them like

towers of green glass, an emerald city. We're off to see the wizard, he shouted. He whooped. His body crouched ready to fly. He shone against the sun. Marina was watching from the sand. She had on a bikini with purple Hawaiian-looking flowers with long yellow stamens. She was eating an ice cream sandwich. She was always eating in those days, West remembered. Her mouth wrapping itself around sweet and creamy or hot and crunchy. She licked her lips and offered him some. He said he was cool. He stood there, trying not to get sand on her towel. She was burning on her shoulders. He wanted to offer to put lotion on her but he didn't. Lex came out of the water and lay down next to her. West just wanted to watch them. He felt the thickness of his wetsuit like he was inside a dolphin. He said he thought he saw some friends he recognized down the beach, maybe he'd catch up with them later, if not he'd see them at school maybe some time.

He avoided them after that. It was just easier.

He didn't know how to handle what he'd felt between them, and what he'd felt for them. There were other pretty girls and ones without brothers like Lex. There were lots of other girls.

Once she was standing by her locker and her puka shells broke and scattered and she made a joke about it but he could tell she was upset. He wanted to buy her some more. He wanted to give her a million strands of little nesting polished shells, and tropical flowers and ice creams and lemonades and a pale blue surfboard to teach her to surf on and anything else she wanted. Instead he let his checkered Vans step on one of the rolling shells and crush it.

So now, who was he, just some guy who she hardly knew. Just another guy that thought she was a fox. Why was he bothering her? She needed time to be alone and get over this thing.

But he couldn't let her alone. He sat with her and asked if she was okay. She said, Yeah, thanks. He said, If you want to talk about it . . .

She nodded, looked down. Her fingers tore at the cuticles on the other hand. She said, Actually I could use a ride this weekend. There's something I gotta check out.

Sure, he said. Trying to act cool. Sure. No problem.

Phases

I ASKED IF I COULD go with you. You said you figured I had plans—it was Saturday night, wasn't it? I said I didn't want to go out with Michelle. I wanted to go with you. You shrugged.

I followed you around the house. You wet your face and head in the sink and shook off the droplets of water and wiped your eyes with the back of your hand and looked at yourself. You weren't wearing a shirt. The mermaid tattoo looked dark and painful against your white skin. You put on your boots and clomped downstairs. You put on one of your albums as loud as you could crank it. My ears hurt but I didn't say anything. I followed you into the kitchen. I felt like a puppy dog. You took a container of milk out of the fridge and guzzled down half of it. A little got on your chin and you wiped it with the back of your hand. You poked at a few food items in there—bologna, white bread, cheese slices, an old apple—and gave up. You went to the bar and filled the flask you kept in your jacket with Bacardi. I could smell the booze drifting up in a little cloud. You put on a T-shirt and a leather jacket and looked at yourself in the mirror panels behind the bar. You said you were ready, let's go. I ran and got my bag. You looked at me quietly. I was wearing a black stretchy top and miniskirt and pumps. I asked if it was okay. You said I looked too pretty for where we were going. I said I didn't know what to wear. You told me, my Levi's. I left on the pumps and the black shirt. I put some black eyeliner on and some silver bracelets.

We left the stereo still blaring on high. You said the album would be over when Mom came home anyway. In the car you played one of your mix tapes. Your car smelled like cigarettes and dirty socks. I opened the windows to let in some air. I tried to smell the ocean far away but all I smelled was the burning tar and smog of the Valley. You lit a cigarette and when I asked for one you said, No way. I pouted but you didn't care. You took the pack and put it in your pocket against your chest. I didn't try to fight you. The cigarette rule was absolute. You always lectured me about them. You said if I got lung cancer and died you were going to kill me. I said what about you? And you said that I could kill you if you died. You glanced at me out of the corner of your eye and asked if I was cold with the wind blowing in on the freeway but I said no. Sometimes when you asked things like that it was like I could feel you touching me with your hand.

We went all the way into the west Valley

where it's more barren, fewer trees, low, identical houses, parking lots. It's darker out there. The streets were empty. The air had a buzzing sound like the neon of liquor store signs.

Phases was this place you always hung out but I'd never been there before. It didn't look like much to me, really. A low building with a neon sign in a parking lot. I remember hearing about this girl, Gina Nichols, who got killed in that parking lot by a drunk driver. She was roller-skating and he hit her. She had a twin sister and after it happened, Mary Nichols started painting her face white and wearing crucifixes and black dresses. I always wondered what it must be like to lose a twin—if somehow Mary felt it like it was happening to her. If she felt physical pain. I heard she was there at the time. I kept thinking about Gina when I saw the parking lot. If you died, I thought, I bet I'd feel it like it was happening to me. That time you had that really high fever I couldn't get out of bed. Mom thought I was faking so I could stay home with you because I didn't have a temperature but I felt so sick. Everything clenching and swirling, my scalp tingling and my ears ringing. And when you broke your wrist skateboarding I was walking home and I swear all of a sudden there was this shooting pain up my arm—before I even knew. At least, I think those things happened. I think so.

There was a clump of girls smoking by this VW and they turned and stared as we pulled in. They had on tight minidresses like the one I'd been wearing and I looked over at you but of course you didn't say anything.

We parked and you sat for a second, staring out through the windshield into the night that was empty and dark except for these lit-up signs for hamburgers and liquor stores. You flattened the butt of your cigarette in the ashtray and raked back what little hair you had with your hand and sighed. You said, Okay, you. You ready?

It was getting a little chilly so you let me wear

your leather jacket (after you removed the pack of cigarettes) and I felt better walking past the girls wearing that. Protection. The girls were checking you out, definitely, and I think you knew them but you hardly acknowledged them. We saw some other girls with big lace-up boots and lots of dark eye makeup. They were wearing black granny dresses with torn T-shirts over them. They had written The Nymphs on the T-shirts in red and black ink. They said hi and you nodded at them. One of them gave me this look like she wanted to deck me which was weird—actually it wasn't weird, the weird part was that I kind of liked it. You saw and leaned down and whispered to me, how was I doing? I smiled up at you. I felt the heat coming off the lining of your jacket and penetrating my skin.

We went inside and sat on one of these carpeted benches around the dance floor and you brought me a Coke, which we spiked with the rum from your bottle. They were playing this new wave music and a few guys and girls were jumping around in the spinning colored lights. They had on bandannas and plastic pop-it beads and low leather boots and striped jeans—new wave stuff like that. You lit a cigarette and said it kind of sucked here tonight. Then you laughed and said actually it always kind of sucked. I asked why you came and you said what else was there to do. You wouldn't look at me when you said that. You said, "I can connect / Nothing with Nothing."

After a while it got more crowded and we were pretty buzzed and then they started playing some punk rock and out of nowhere all these guys were on the dance floor slamming around and going crazy. They had shaved heads and tattoos and T-shirts that said Fiend on them, handwritten. You got up and joined them. I got scared because it looked like when you got out there they started banging harder into you but you were strong and taller than most of them. I wanted to jump in, too. I wanted to feel the thud of bodies crashing into me. I could feel myself shaking to the music. I took off your leather jacket because I could feel the sweat trickling down my sides, smelling like baby powder and Bacardi. When you came back your hair was slick with sweat.

One of the guys from out there came over. He had a rat tattooed on his arm, the tail tracing up his forearm over the biggest vein there. He had a jagged look, like every part of him would hurt. His eyes were the coldest film of ice. He said hey, asked you who I was. You asked him why he wanted to know. He flashed his sharp teeth at you. He said why'd you think? because I was a babe. You said I was your sister and you looked like a statue. He said, Hello, Lex's sister. You said we were going to leave, you had to get me home early. He said he'd be seeing me.

As we walked away you mumbled like hell he would. You said he was psychotic, like certified, with guns in the basement and shit and I better make sure I stayed away from him. You said you should never have brought me. I wanted to say I was glad you did but I was afraid you'd be mad.

We stopped at Dupar's on the way home. The creamy swirly pies and cakes were reflected in mirrors so it looked like they were attached to the walls against gravity. The decor was bright and yellow and orange and fifties. The waitresses wore starched uniforms and big starched hairdos, big frilly napkins in their breast pockets. They were grumpy and suspicious of us. We sat in a vinyl booth and ate our pie. There were a few drunks, a couple of kids, a punk with a bad complexion being spoon-fed ice cream by two giggling women who looked like porn actresses. We started to laugh. It was so easy being with you at that moment. It was so easy.

Nymph

I CUT SCHOOL *and went to see the nymph. It was too hot to breathe. The sky was yellow and smelled of sulphur. The pool in the apartment building had been drained. I thought of skateboarding in the pit and cracking my skull.*

We got high in her parents' room. She said her mother had stopped fucking her stepfather after the last kid. Now when he drank too much, he tried his daughter's bed. She said she'd started sleeping with a switchblade. She said that pain helps you see everyone else's really clearly. Or it makes you blind.

She said, What do you want me to be? Do you want me to be her? Blond wig? Some puka shells and cutoffs. It's not my style but whatever.

I said, No, no. Gargoyles and demons. Succubus.

Kinky, she said.

I said, Get on my chest. Crouch on my chest. Like that painting. You know. The dream. That thing is on the woman's chest. Suck the life out of me.

She said, Oh, I get it. So you want me to punish you? You want me to call you bad boy? Is that it? What did you do that was so bad, boy?

She was the farthest I could get from you. That's what I wanted.

WEST PICKED MARINA UP at ten. She was standing outside smoking. There was a burned smell in the air, like the red oleander flowers in front of her house were on fire. The red stoplight. Her red lipstick and her red rhinestone necklace were on fire. She didn't say much when she got into his Mustang. She put out the cigarette and started biting her nails.

West asked if she was okay. She asked if he wanted the real answer or the lie. He said real, always real, and she said she was shitty. He was quiet for a long time as they drove down Laurel to the 101. Rodney on KROQ was playing some local punk bands. West told Marina that he was sorry for asking her like that, making her say how she was when how else could she be. He felt even stupider after that but she thanked him. She thanked him for coming to the funeral. It was weird, she said, she knew Lex wouldn't have wanted a funeral like that but her mom wouldn't listen. She said he'd want to be cremated and have his ashes scattered over the ocean. She opened the window and put her head out and let the warm Santa Anas rush into her hair like a million wild fingers, loving her. He wished they could keep going past the Valley exit, head out to Topanga and take it west to the ocean, or circle onto the 405 and then the 10 to Santa Monica. Any way she wanted just so they could have water and sand. He would wrap her in blankets and build a fire and show her stars because she should have stars, he thought. All over her body like jewelry.

Instead they were going to this crappy club in the middle of nowhere where she wanted to go to find something that had to do with Lex when the real Lex was probably where his ashes should have been scattered.

Hyacinth Girl

IF **MR. MONTGOMERY** wasn't going out of town and hadn't asked you to house-sit for him maybe it wouldn't have happened. Maybe. Wine and paintings and old books and a Spanish house with windows over a sunken garden. Maybe it would have happened anyway.

Mr. Montgomery was the only teacher you got along with. He thought you had talent as a writer. I only know this because he told me. He stopped me in the hall and asked me into his classroom. He introduced himself formally, even though I knew who he was, of course, and he said you were in his class and he thought you were going to be an important writer someday. He said he was telling me because he was afraid you wouldn't tell me what he'd said and that he thought you should have all the support you could get at home. I said that I'd never read anything you'd written but that you were always reading like a demon. He liked the expression *reading-demon*. He asked if I wrote, too, and I said no. He asked if I kept a journal. I didn't, then. I decided I might try. He said you'd written this great paper on this poem called "The Waste Land" and that I should ask you to see it. Maybe it would help me when I got into his class next year. He smiled like he was looking forward to that. I thanked him. I'd always kind of liked Mr. Montgomery from afar. He always seemed like one of the coolest teachers. People whispered that he was gay and that he hung out at a gay bar called Oil Can Harry's but because he was so nice and good-looking and cool it never seemed to really hurt him which was a big deal at our school where the littlest thing like a wandering eye or flood pants or some zits made kids start persecuting you like crazy.

I came home and asked you about your paper. I told you what Mr. Montgomery had said. You didn't say anything but I could tell you were secretly pleased and flattered that he'd told me. You said the paper was just some bullshit but I made you show it to me. It was all about fragmentation in the modern world. Modern meaning not now but way back in the twenties when it was written. But you said it still applied. The loss of God. Postmodernism being just a further breakdown and kind of an empty term as of yet in your opinion. You quoted "I can connect / Nothing with Nothing." You called me the hyacinth girl. You read some lines and I didn't understand any of it. You sounded like the homeless man who wanders on Ventura Boulevard eating out of trash cans and mumbling to himself.

But it was kind of beautiful, beautiful and strange. Like the homeless man with hyacinth blue eyes that shine out of his char-dark face. You said I was the hyacinth girl. "Yet when we came back, late, from the Hyacinth garden / Your arms full, and your hair wet, I could not / Speak, and my eyes failed. I was neither / Living nor dead, and I knew nothing, / Looking into the heart of light, the silence, / *Oed' und leer das Meer*." Desolate and empty the sea, you said.

I told mom I was staying at Michelle's but instead I went over to Mr. Montgomery's house. He lived in the Hollywood Hills south and east of the Valley. It felt so different around there— bohemian, old, and rambling. I wondered what it would be like if we got a house there someday. An old Spanish house like Mr. Montgomery's with a thick cool adobe wall covered with crispy bougainvillea flowers and a sunken garden with a stone fountain and broad tall windows. You opened the big wooden door and let me in. Inside there were polished wood floors and high beams and lots of ironwork, painted wooden furniture, framed silk kimonos, primitive stone statues. You handed me a huge goblet of wine. I asked if it was okay and you said there was so much wine he wouldn't even notice. He said to make myself at home, you said. There wasn't just a lot of wine, but a lot a lot of books. The walls were solid books. A lot of them were old ones with fragile leather covers and golden lettering. You opened one so that I could smell it. You said old books smelled cool. A pressed leaf fell out and you put it back in carefully. Some of the books were dedicated to Ned from Joel. You said Joel was Mr. Montgomery's boyfriend and that he was way nice, too, and that you'd met him for a second when you came over to get the key. You said you thought it was weird that they trusted you enough to stay in their house but I said it must have been because what you wrote was so good. You said you wouldn't have trusted you based on that.

You had made a fire in the deep fireplace with the Spanish tiles all around it and we sat there and drank our wine and ate some cheese, crackers, pickles, and canned mandarin oranges you had found. We played Mr. Montgomery's classical records which you said sounded cool in this environment. You read to me from some of the books. Emily Dickinson and Walt Whitman. We looked at the paintings on the walls. They were by someone with the initials J.S. and we wondered if it was Mr. Montgomery's boyfriend Joel. They were big oil paintings of figures dancing and twining around each other. The colors seemed to pulse. It was like a single person with lots of limbs, a male and female all in one like Tiresias who is in that "Waste Land" poem. You found a James Brown record and played that. We took off our shoes and skidded around on the polished floors. We got drunk and poked around the house and went into the walk-in closet and tried on some of Mr. Montgomery and Joel's jackets. I used some of their cologne. Then I wanted to take a bath so I ran water into the big sunken tub and poured in some bath salts and lit the candles in the square glass holders around the rim of the tub. There were big windows overlooking the garden. I opened them and smelled the jasmine and the wet earth. There was a little warm breeze and the garden tinkled and chimed like stars falling. I called you. I wanted a refill on my wine. I wanted to give you the jasmine and the wind chime stars.

I'm sorry.

Fragments

I REMEMBER THE HEAT *singing like crickets, the cold beer can crushed in my hand—how razor-sharp the place I drank from—the laughter tumbling like your hair. I remember the blue flowers in your hair. You showed me the way their blood was glue, clinging to you by themselves.*

Try not to think of you. Think of Michelle with granulated sugar on her lips, eating raw cookie dough, Michelle sliding the comb out of her jeans. Your bedroom door was open. I pretended not to watch you and Michelle combing each other's hair, tying each other's bikini tops, oiling each other's backs.

Try not to think of your sunburned shoulders peeling little bits of flesh like insect wings, your legs on the dashboard, the hair on them glinting, the sand on your toes.

Try to think of boots crunching glass, skeletons of ice, skin of white, Rat with his bullet pupils, Justine's mouth like a black crucifix.

Try not to think of Death.
Try not to think.
Try not to.
Try not.

Kill

YOU SAID, You know that guy, Rat, from Phases? He may have a basement of artillery but believe me if he ever comes near you I am going to kill him. I said, Don't talk like that. He doesn't give a fuck about me. You said I didn't know him. He'd kill somebody for a lot less than trying to sleep with a girl he liked. But you'd kill him first. I said, Lex, stop it. I wanted to take you in my arms like a little boy and stroke your bristly head but I knew that I could never touch you again.

WEST AND MARINA PULLED into the parking lot where Gina Nichols had been roller-skating when the drunk driver hit her. There were a few kids hanging out. The air smelled like french fries—batter and grease. The sky looked empty of planets. It felt like nothing existed except this building reverberating with music you couldn't name.

West wondered why someone as cool as Lex came here. It was like nothing. Maybe that was why, West thought. You want nothing when you are trying to forget the something that is everything. He looked over at Marina but he couldn't read her face.

She got out fast and he followed her across the lot to the door where the biker bouncer took their money. She went to the ladies room and came back with fresh lipstick and smelling like vanilla and flowers that bloom at night. She didn't want a drink. He bought two Cokes anyway and after a while she started sipping it. She kept looking around nervously, like she was trying to find someone.

It got late and West would have almost asked her to dance. They played pretty good music. A Siouxsie and the Banshees song. He almost asked her but he didn't want to seem like a geek.

It got later and just when he thought she was about to ask if they could go this pack of punk guys came in, swaggering like they owned the place, West thought. They spread out and surveyed the scene, one of them told the D.J. something and the next song was hard core—they were all over the dance floor slamming, which seemed pretty lame to West at a place like this rather than in a pit at a gig, but what did he know? He noticed Marina staring at them and when the song was over she got up and walked over to a sinewy guy with spiky bleached hair and a handsome, depraved-looking face. In the black lights his pale eyes shone. He grinned and his teeth glowed, too.

West didn't know if she'd appreciate what he did, but he knew Lex would have and besides he felt like he had to do something so he went over there. The guy turned to him and said, Isn't she a babe? All chicks should look like this. Don't you think all chicks should look like this? West didn't know what to say. Who's this guy? the guy asked Marina. My friend. Not your boyfriend, though, right? I mean, your brother was such a fuckin' guard dog. He wouldn't even let me talk to her, he told West. But I guess now that isn't really a problem, is it, dude?

Let's go, West said to Marina. She nodded but she kept staring at the guy like there was something more she wanted.

Later, he said, grinning at her, his eyeballs like pale swirly marbles in the darkness. He tapped his front tooth with one long jagged pinky fingernail.

When they got outside she was shivering, even though it was still warm, and West made her wear his army jacket. He asked her what that was all about. She said that guy knew Lex and she wanted to ask him a few questions. West said, What a freak, and she nodded and peeled off some more fingernail polish with her teeth. He asked if she wanted to go somewhere for a hot chocolate or something and she stopped biting her nails and looked at him. She said softly, Hot chocolate? And he shrugged, embarrassed. He said, I don't know. Whatever. You looked cold. She thanked him. She said hot chocolate was a great suggestion but she was tired. She said he was too nice to her and she was fucked up and he should probably find some sane girl to buy hot chocolate for. He asked if she were saying that to be nice, to get rid of him, because if that was it he'd never bother her again. She was so quiet and when she looked at him her eyes were red and wet—he thought of crumpled tissue. He knew the answer, so when he dropped her off he said he'd give her a call. She leaned over and kissed his cheek. Every hair on his body stood at attention and he felt swept into the warm wind that blasted him when she got out of the car. He was lying on the horizon—his body was the mountain and his hair was the Santa Anas and his eyes were planets. He couldn't go home so he drove up to Mulholland where Marty Fallbrook had crashed his moped and died and he parked and looked across the seething lights of the Valley and knew she was down there, sleeping, and tried to find her scent of smoke and cookies and flowers on the wind.

Cruel Thing

THERE WAS THIS GIRL named Dana Dell
and she was going out with Jeff Glasser. Dana
Dell: really tall, long straight blond hair, big
breasts, all the guys love her. Kind of snobby but
not that bad. Jeff Glasser is shorter than Dana,
and good-looking except he is so mean that it
ruins it in my opinion. In junior high he used to
call some of the girls dogs and draw pictures of
them and things like that. Hold up pieces of
paper with numbers written on them, rating the
girls as they went by. Jeff Glasser—a real prince.
He told Candy Pierce that she'd be cute—if
someone cut off her head. The next semester she

came back looking completely different. She'd had some radical plastic surgery that had changed the whole shape of her forehead and jaw, besides just her nose and eyelids. It always made my face hurt to look at her.

I don't know why Dana Dell went out with Jeff Glasser at all but after she broke up with him he covered the whole side of the math building with this graffiti that said: Dana D. is a whore. Everyone knew it was Jeff Glasser who did it but he didn't get caught. Dana took it pretty badly, which surprised me, really. Because she seemed pretty tough. But people were laughing at her and guys were hissing things in the halls and some of her girlfriends used the whole thing as an excuse to dump her from their clique, the Puffs, because they'd always been jealous of her anyway. (Candy Pierce was one of them.) Lots of other girls wanted to be friends with her and a lot of guys still liked her but she changed schools.

Melvins were when they caught the nerdy

boys and pulled up their pants to their chests. There were kids who got pushed or beaten or just laughed at which could be just as bad when you were trying to grow up as invisibly as possible. Girls who got goosed in the ass so hard it bruised. (If they complained they were told by the V.P. not to wear jeans that you had to lie down to zip.) A lot of this stuff stopped happening after junior high, but it didn't really go away. It just got subtler. The same kids and the memories of what they'd done ruled us.

So I always wondered what would have happened if anyone found out about you and me. I guess I wouldn't have cared that much but I think you would have gone crazy and maybe killed somebody if they said anything to me. I mean really killed somebody.

Or maybe someone did find out.

It ENDED UP that Marina called West. She was apologizing and crying and he couldn't understand her so he asked if he should come over and she said yes.

When he got there he followed her into her room. It was just the way he'd imagined it—cluttered and sweet and still more like a little girl's than a young woman's. There were stuffed animals and a little bed with a flowered bedspread—but when she sat down he saw it sloshed and realized it was a waterbed. He sat on a little chair and waited. She thanked him for coming and apologized again for how she was on the phone. She said something had really freaked her out and she didn't know who to talk to about it.

The thing that had happened was a girl had come to Marina's door. It was one of the punk girls from the funeral, Justine. She said she was a friend of Lex's and that she wanted to make a shrine to him and she needed some materials. She wanted mementos, anything Marina could spare. Marina said she couldn't do that and the girl got pissed off. She kept insisting. Marina said, No, please leave, and the girl spat on the front doorstep. She said that Marina would regret this. She said that it's one thing to keep someone to yourself when they are alive, but when they are dead it's really sick.

I didn't even know her, Marina said. I didn't know what she was talking about.

West watched Marina bobbing on the waterbed, gripping the covers like a storm was coming.

The next day she got this note, she said. It was in the mailbox. She handed it to him—scrawled on a torn piece of paper, written with dark lipstick. It said: Incest is Best.

What the fuck? West said.

Marina said, She wrote it. Then she said, Nothing happened. It's not what you think.

I don't think anything, said West. I don't know anything. But he wanted to do something, anything that would make it a little better.

Let's get out of here, he said. Let's go to the beach.

They took Topanga, which was deep and green and winding and where no one they knew had died. West's parents had been married there, though, at a terraced garden restaurant with fountains and heat lamps and clusters of white roses like little wedding cakes and statues of St. Francis, Buddha, Mary, and Krishna. They still liked to go there for brunch and West pretended he was bored but actually he liked it. He would have liked to take Marina there sometime but he didn't want to seem lame. Cool guys didn't take girls to places like that. Probably not. But it was all right to drive through the canyon and tell her (somewhat cynically) about his parents' funky wedding and she seemed to like that. They were hippies? she said, and he kind of balked so she added that she thought it was cool. He said his parents were pretty cool, actually. They weren't hippies anymore. They were both architects and had their own firm. They built geodesic domes and things like that. Marina said it was amazing he had parents who were still together—almost nobody did. She asked why they still lived in the Valley. West laughed. He said they kept asking the same thing, they were trying to move to Santa Monica.

West drove out onto Pacific Coast Highway, out of the dark trees green and into ocean glitter blue. He heard Marina take a deep breath for what seemed like the first time that day. He said, That time I came here with you and Lex, that was cool, and then he wished he hadn't brought Lex up but she didn't seem to mind. She said, Yeah, that was way fun. You surfed so great. I was blown away. West felt so happy at that moment. He felt like if he went out now he wouldn't even need a surfboard. He could just walk on the waves.

But he didn't surf that day. They just sat on the sand in their clothes and talked. They took walks and met puppies. They waded around the tide pools and found shells. She loved the abalone best—all the swirling oily rainbows inside the coarse exterior. She built a sandcastle and he added a feather on top of one of the turrets but otherwise he wouldn't participate—he had to draw the line somewhere with these things to preserve some kind of image, right? When the sun started to go down they sat on a rock and watched the orange flaming sky, the sand made into a mirror reflecting the strutting gulls. They talked some more. They talked about school and music and surfing and stuff. Nothing much. But it felt like they were telling each other secrets. Everything they said felt like that—whispered, tender, full of other meanings, like when you tell someone a dream or talk about your astrological signs as code for all the things you love about each other. West remembered the first time he listened to an album by himself. It was *Clouds* by Joni Mitchell. He was lying on the floor with his head next to the speaker and the volume really low so he wouldn't wake his mom and dad. Listening to Marina felt like that.

On the way home they stopped for burritos and chips and lemonade which they had in the car while they drove, listening to the Ventures. Twanging riffs of surf guitar. Marina put her bare sandy feet up on the dashboard. She hadn't shaved her legs and the soft golden hairs gleamed against her gold skin. She had delicate, articulate toes that reminded him of cat's paws when she flexed them. She had a thin silver chain around one thin golden ankle. When she realized how she was sitting she slid her feet down and apologized and sat up. They were back on the freeway going into the Valley by that time. He said she was fine like she was, but he could tell the spell of the day was broken. She was remembering what she had left behind.

He said, What are you looking for?

She turned her face away and he knew she was crying. He put his hand on her shoulder. It felt bony, jutting under the cotton and fleece. Fuck, she said, rolling her eyes up as she turned back to him, dabbing at tears with the sweatshirt sleeve she had pulled down over her hand like a paw. Here I go again.

He said, It's okay. Then: Just tell me.

Marina looked at him but in a way he felt she wasn't seeing him there. She was talking to a phantom—an invisible dead boy. She said, I don't believe he killed himself. I don't believe it. Something's not right about it. Lex didn't mess around with guns.

West didn't think that was what she was going to tell him. He'd never questioned that Lex had killed himself. He thought Marina was looking for why and that she already knew the answer and he thought he did, too, but she wasn't ready to confront it yet.

But he said—softly, because she was like a sleepwalker who you don't want to wake suddenly for fear of traumatizing them—What do you think happened?

I don't know, she said, still asleep, still sleeptalking to her ghost. I'm trying to find out.

West didn't want her to get hurt anymore. He wanted her to let go. He wanted her to appreciate her life. To know he loved her. All these things sounded so stupid to him when he imagined saying them and he knew she didn't want to hear them anyway. She wanted to hear one thing.

I'll help you, he said.

That was when she saw him again. For a moment the ghost was gone and she just saw him, West, holding her in his eyes.

The Garden

NOTHING HAPPENED. And everything did. Your whole life you can be told something is wrong and so you believe it. Why should you question it? But then slowly seeds are planted inside of you, one by one, by a touch or a look or a day skateboarding in a park, and they start to unfurl uncurl little green shoots and they start to burst out of old hulls shells and they start to sprout. And pretty soon there are so many of them. They are named Love and Trust and Kindness and Joy and Desire and Wonder and Spirit and Soulmate. They grow into a garden so dense and thick that it starts to invade your brain where the old things you were once told are dying. By the time this garden reaches your brain the old things are dead. They make no sense. The logic of the seeds sprouted inside of you is the only real thing.

That was what happened to us, wasn't it? It was like when we were little kids and we played games on the ivy-covered hillside in the backyard. We were warriors and wizards and angels and high elves and that was our reality. If someone said, Isn't it cute, look at them playing, we would have smiled back, humoring them, but it wasn't playing. It was transformation. It was our own world. Our own rules.

And the same thing happened that night.

We were in Mr. Montgomery and Joel's bedroom. We were drinking Mr. Montgomery and Joel's wine out of the bottle by that time. The painting of the creature that was male and female with many arms and legs was shimmering thick rose and tourmaline and cocoa and cream shades of oil paint dancing above us. We tried on some of Ned (he was Ned by that time) and Joel's clothes. I used some cologne that smelled dry and cool and sage. I decided to take a bath.

When I called you in my heart started to pound so hard I thought it would jump out of the water like a fish. I wondered if you would catch it in your big hands. You started to hum the *Jaws* music and I pretended to be scared because of that.

You weren't wearing a shirt because you had been trying on Ned and Joel's shirts earlier. I looked at the segments of your stomach. You took off your sweats and slid into the water. I screamed, pretending it was because you were Jaws. We were little kids in the tub rub-a-dub-dub playing a game.

We got quiet. The garden was combing her hair and putting on her earrings. The house was full of dancing creatures, not male not female but both, two lovers in one body. The books downstairs were reciting their poetry to each other, rubbing together, whispering through the leather covers. Wine was flowing through the water pipes. You had caught my leaping heart in your hand like a fish.

WEST TOOK MARINA BACK to Phases even though he wished that she would stop going there. He didn't understand how it was going to help her. She was wearing Lex's leather jacket and no makeup and her hair looked like she had chopped it herself. It was full of pinkish gel that smelled like strawberries.

It was pretty much like the other time but then that Rat guy came in with his pack of friends. Marina said Lex had names for all of them—Mole Man, Toast, Zombie. West laughed because he could tell exactly who was who. Lex could really call it. Mole wore a hooded sweat-

90

shirt and looked like he never went out in the day. Toast was sunburnt and his eyes looked fried on acid. Zombie was huge and staggering. When Marina went over to Rat the others moved away. West watched, trying to figure out what she was saying. He knew it wasn't good. She was smiling and touching her hair and she didn't back away when Rat leaned in close to light her cigarette. He wanted to rush to her but he made himself sit still. She had asked him to let her do this. And West knew she was faking, too. He knew her real smile too well by now. After all those days watching it across the quad, in the hallways, in yearbooks— trying to catch it like a butterfly.

But when she kept talking and he could tell where it was going he wasn't sure he could let it. He started to get up but she was coming over to him. She said, I have to go, I'm sorry, West. It's just this once. I have to find some stuff out. Don't worry.

Let me go with you, he said. It was the most

he'd ever said to her. He felt like he had told her part of the secret he'd had since the day he'd seen her in her puka shells with her brother.

She didn't touch him but she looked at him like she wanted to and she said she was sorry. Please. Just this once. She walked away.

West waited until they walked out of the club. Then he got up and followed them.

He parked down the street and watched Marina and Rat get out of the green Plymouth. He watched her trying to light another cigarette and Rat stopping and helping her maybe because her hands were shaking, although West couldn't see that far. She looked young and small to him, suddenly, even though he wasn't much taller. She looked like somebody's little sister.

They went behind the house which was low and beige cottage cheese and almost windowless. They didn't go into the house but around behind it. West waited a little while and then followed them. There was a separate back entrance and West crept across the sparse yellow grass that smelled of dog piss up to one of the few windows and looked in.

The light was dim but he saw walls sound-proofed with burnt orange shag carpeting, a mess of beer bottles, a drum set, scattered news-papers and fanzines, furniture covered with graffiti. He saw Rat open a small fridge and pop two Coors, hand one to Marina, slam down the other. She sat on the brown sofa that looked like it had been picked up on a curb. Stuffing was coming out and it was missing some cushions. Rat stood facing her with his arms crossed over his chest, one hip cocked. He wasn't drinking the beer. He was watching her.

Marina laughed nervously, touching her strawberry-gelled self-chopped hair. What? she said.

Rat said, I'm just trying to figure something out.

She didn't say anything.

Why'd you come here with me? You left your little buddy back there pretty upset.

He's just my friend, Marina said. And West felt his incisors dig into his lip.

Okay. So why'd you want to come home with me? To fuck?

Marina laughed again, high and out of breath. Maybe I should go, she said, standing up.

Rat came and faced her. West saw him from the back, his narrow hips and hard belligerent ass and spiky hair, the bulge of his biceps in the thin T-shirt. For a second West wondered if she was here for that, if she'd been messing with his head.

Rat took her small chin in his hand. He brought her face close to his. West felt adrenaline pounding in his body like a drug. Injected.

Rat made her sit on the couch. He sat next to her.

Rat said, in a softer voice, Then what?

I don't know. I just knew you knew my

brother. And you know I'm just trying to talk to some people who knew him.

Rat nodded. He flicked ashes onto the floor, then dropped his cigarette and snuffed it with his steel-toed boot like he was killing a bug. You wanted to talk about your big brother?

Marina shrugged. She said, I don't know. I should probably get going.

When she tried to stand he grabbed her wrist and pulled her back down.

She didn't fight his grip but she stared into his face, like she wasn't afraid anymore, like she had nothing to lose. (Did she feel she had nothing to lose? West wondered.)

Did you sell my brother a gun? Marina said.

A little detective, Rat said. Is that it?

What?

If you're looking for what happened to him you're looking in the wrong place. You should be looking a lot closer to home. You should be looking for a girl, first of all.

Then Rat started to laugh, wheezing and coughing and slapping his knees.

Marina got up and walked out of the room as if she weren't scared as hell. As if she had nothing to lose.

Rat said, You really shouldn't let yourself go like that. You used to be pretty hot.

As she walked out West said her name softly, so as not to scare her. She whirled around and he got the feeling she had expected someone else—a ghost, maybe, a specific ghost, the ghost of a tall boy who looked like a young Jim Morrison with short hair. But she looked like she was glad it was West, anyway. She didn't question that he was there. She took his hand when he held it out to her and they ran to the car.

He felt like shit that he hadn't done anything. His big rescue mission. What? He'd watched her through a window, biting his mouth until there was blood. Big deal. Big fuckin' hero. Still, she kept thanking him for being there. She said he was her guardian angel. She said it was like someone had sent him to her to protect her.

West knew she meant Lex. He wondered if she were thanking Lex instead of him and then he told himself that if Lex had gotten him there, at least she was with him now, at least she was safe.

They drove up to Mulholland where people went to make love in their cars but West and Marina didn't touch each other. They sat and watched the lights shining in the basin because they couldn't look at each other (for different reasons) and because they couldn't see any stars. He asked her why she had gone there with that guy and she said she knew she owed West an explanation but he might not understand. He said, Try me.

She told him that she really did feel like there was something not right about how Lex died, that maybe someone else had been involved. She said she had suspected Rat because he was such a loose cannon, and because of the guns Lex had told her about. But there really wasn't a motivation, was there? And then Rat had said this thing about a girl and she wanted to know who that was. She said she knew she sounded crazy—she couldn't help it. Maybe she was crazy.

West wasn't sure what to say so he just shook his head like, no, you are not crazy, and sat with her, quietly, the way his mom used to do when he was scared. Finally he said, You knew him better than anyone.

Who is this girl? she said, talking to the ghost boy again. West wondered when he'd come back, if he were hovering on the hood of the car, staring at her through the windows.

I mean, he didn't seem like he hung around anybody much. Except me and Michelle.

When she said her friend's name she started groping around in her pink vinyl bag for a cigarette. Her mouth looked small and tense like it was already inhaling smoke.

West had been wondering for a long time, so he asked her, Where's Michelle been lately anyway? Meaning, Why wasn't she at the funeral, but of course he didn't say that.

We had a fight, Marina said.

Blind

I DIDN'T THINK *you were in there.*

Didn't I?

You stopped where you stood and pulled the towel around you. You didn't look angry or scared. Your eyes looked the way they did when I came to you in your crib when you were a baby.

I turned away but I knew. That your eyes were still watching me that way, the time I came to you in your crib. Almost as if you had been calling me.

I wished you had struck me blind.

After that, it started. I knew too much. I couldn't stop seeing you standing there like that. To make it stop I went to Michelle. But nothing happened. I couldn't. I don't know what's wrong with me.

I had to go into your room when you weren't there. I'm sorry. I had to open drawers and touch things. It was the only way. Do you understand? I don't expect you to. But it was the only way. I'm sorry.

Maybe I thought it would make me understand. What you feel. I didn't want to take anything from you. Did I?

Girls

I<small>T WASN'T</small> M<small>ICHELLE'S FAULT</small>. And I'm not mad at you anymore. You needed to do something that would break what we had, make it possible to live with it. It didn't work.

After the night at Mr. Montgomery's house (he was Mr. Montgomery again) you changed. You wouldn't look into my eyes. You locked your door. You locked yourself. You called Michelle.

I don't know why you had to pick her. You could have chosen Megan Warren who won "best eyes," or Lisa Henderson who is the only girl at our school to bleach her hair white and wear vintage dresses with pointed satin pumps, and who can play bass and may be starting an all-girl band, or Teresa Villanova who used to come to your track meets and has legs almost as long as yours and can fly when she runs. You could have chosen anyone and it would have been easier.

I told myself, it makes sense. Why wouldn't Michelle want to go out with you? Why wouldn't you want to go out with her? I remembered all those times the three of us spent together. I wondered if you were waiting for her all those times. To try and comfort myself I made up something. I told myself that you chose Michelle less because of her Brooke Shields eyebrows and dark brown legs and shiny hair (that she hadn't chopped off because you said punk was cool) or because of how nice she was to Marty Fallbrook or because of how quiet she was, smiling mysteriously as the Mona Lisa, and more because of how close her body had come to mine—dancing at Kaleidoscope in our spandex pants and Candie's slip-ons when we were fourteen, cuddling on the lawn chair on New Year's Eve when we were twelve, making chocolate chip cookie dough and eating it all raw and lying on your bed moaning in pain until you kicked us out when we were ten. Or maybe you chose Michelle for all those reasons. And because of how much it hurt.

She called me laughing and excited and saying it was so crazy after all these years, she'd never have expected it. Lex! She said something about that time we were little and you saw us in our underwear and how mortified she was. She said, It might be weird. I mean he's almost like a brother.

I thought it was going to be okay. But then she said, You won't believe it, Marina. I've had a crush on him forever. I never wanted to tell you because I thought I'd sound stupid. I never thought he'd like me. I thought he'd pick someone who could write poetry and look good bald.

That was when I turned into a bitch. I said I knew what she meant. I'd have figured you'd have picked someone from Oakwood, the artsy private school down the street, someone really smart and experienced and unique. Sophisticated, I think I said. I might have said, mature.

Michelle laughed because she wasn't used to me being mean to her—ever. She said, Thanks, Marina!

I said, No, I'm just saying. I was a little surprised myself. I said I had to go. I said, See ya.

Like, Luv ya, stay as sweet as you are, have a great summer! written in round cursive letters in a yearbook. See ya.

Or not.

I stopped calling Michelle and even after what happened happened I couldn't talk to her. What could I say? She sent a condolence card to me and Mom but she didn't come to the funeral.

I WONDER IF the girl is that one who wanted me to give her something of his, Marina said. To the ghost.

THE GIRL WASN'T AT PHASES but her friends were—the ones who had been with her at the funeral crying louder that anyone, louder that Lex's sister who hadn't cried at all. Marina told West she was going to talk to them. This time he made her wait. He said, You wanted my help. I can't just sit here. And this time she let him go with her.

The girls all had dyed-black hair that smelled sticky-sweet and flammable with hair spray. Their faces were white with powder and they were all dressed in black. West was surprised at how much Marina looked like one of them except for her hair. He hadn't realized how much she'd changed since he'd first seen her. And how little it mattered to him.

The girls weren't too happy to see her, even with her chopped hair and black leather jacket. They gave her a look like she was one of the new wave girls in a pastel camouflage minidress.

Marina said, How's it going?

Usually this charmed people, West knew. The easy way she spoke, no affect, almost more like a guy. The girls weren't buying, though.

Your friend? she said. Is she coming tonight?

Why do you want to know? the tall girl asked.

I have something for her.

This didn't seem to interest them until Marina said, For her altar.

The plumpest, prettiest girl said, She told us you were extremely rude about that.

Marina seemed ready for this response. I guess I was, kind of. I was still really upset about what happened.

The girls exchanged looks that West didn't particularly like.

Well, she's not coming tonight.

Could you tell me how to get in touch with her?

We'll give it to her.

Marina smiled again. Thanks a lot. I just would rather do it myself.

She stroked the thick, cracked sleeves of the leather jacket suggestively and the girls' plucked eyebrows went up.

I get the feeling she's really an artist, Marina said. I thought she could do something meaningful. I think Lex would really want her to have it.

I'll tell her to come see you, the girl with the pierced nose said.

West was over at Marina's watching TV when Justine did come. She had perfect skin and high cheekbones, a pouting mouth. Unlike her friends, who seemed to be hiding under their makeup and hair and clothes, she used hers to say, I can look awesome without any of your conventional prettygirly shit. She had shaved her head since the time West had seen her and it was covered with dark stubble. He had to admit she could carry it off, but when he looked at her he felt something like black wings stirring his gut.

Marina thanked her for coming and invited her in. Justine just stared at her with her arms folded on her chest and her mouth pout.

I'm sorry if I was weird to you last time, Marina said. I was still kind of in shock.

I heard you had something for me, Justine said.

Yeah. I do have something. You can come in if you want. She put on the high-beam smile and Justine reluctantly shrugged her way through the door as if she were taking off a sweater she hated.

They went into the den, because, West was pretty sure, Marina didn't want to be sitting under the pictures of herself, her mom, and Lex. Justine had already noticed them and stopped to stare at ten-year-old Lex with hair in his eyes.

West went to get diet sodas, which was all there was. When he came back, they were sitting on the couch and Marina was saying, What's this project?

I believe I already told you, Justine said, as if there were periods between all the words. I believe you were so impressed with it you agreed to donate something. Because I'm such an artist? That's what I heard, anyway?

Marina laughed and thanked West for the drink. I just wanted to hear more about it, she said.

Listen, let's cut the crap, okay? I cared for your brother and I would like to express my feelings by making something. If you want to help me that would be great. It might even help you get over some of your guilt.

Excuse me, Marina said. He could see a tiny snarl starting in her lip.

Justine's sleepy slouchy manner suddenly changed. She sat up and pushed the soda away from her. I really liked Lex, okay! And if somebody hadn't come between us the whole thing might have turned out very differently, okay!

What the hell are you talking about?

West went and sat next to Marina. She pressed the toes of her left foot into the ground and her leg shook. He remembered her trembling body the day she'd heard about her brother.

Get over yourself, Justine said. Marina followed her out of the brown velour den, through the shiny pale blue crystal dining room, into the front of the house with the pictures of a young Lex and Marina smiling down from the wall with baby teeth.

What's your fucking problem? What did you do to my brother?

Fuck you! Justine yelled, slamming the tall

door so that the whole room seemed to shake like an earthquake had just passed through.

Maybe it had, West thought.

Or maybe it had just started.

Boys

WHEN I WAS LITTLE I followed you around everywhere you went. I never let you out of my sight if possible. I cried hysterically when you had to go away to school or Little League or whatever. I begged Mom to let me go with you. I tried to walk and talk like you and wear boys' clothes so that it would be easier to smuggle myself into the life you had away from mine. You never got mad at me or acted embarrassed when I tagged along. I think if you could have you would have taken me everywhere. You showed me off proudly, even when other boys teased. Marina, show 'em how you skateboard.

Or when I was really little, If I put my finger in her dimple it'll get stuck, I swear. Better not try it. You never let anyone else touch me if you could help it. You touched me way more than Mom ever did, I know that. Although she was always holding and cuddling you. When she did you looked worried. You glanced over at me to make sure I was okay. You wriggled out of her arms to run away and play with me.

I never looked at other boys. I tried, as I got older, to like them. I tried to like my square-dance partner in sixth grade graduation, Dave Alden, but he was shorter than I was and smelled like a pink rubber handball after a game when the grime comes off in your palms. I tried teen idols with their skinny bodies and girly hair and whiny voices. I liked Jim Morrison but only in the early days when he looked like you so I figured that didn't count. I tried to like Robby Rydell from afar because he was a good skateboarder and acted cool but he caught me with a jump-rope lasso and tried to stick his tongue in my mouth on the playground before he ever said hi. I really tried hard to like Brent Fisher because it seemed important that I find somebody at that point. Not somebody to fill a space. There was never a space.

I shut my eyes in bed at night and tried to see myself with Brent Fisher. I made up boys based on ones I'd seen in surf magazines and the movies. Ocean hair, sky eyes, bare skin, sweat, salt. All I could think of was you.

We never talked about people we had crushes on or things like that. Until Michelle.

At one point I tried to talk about boys with you to see if I'd get a reaction. You just ignored me which worked because I stopped.

Only once, you mentioned a boy. You said, That kid, West, what's-his-name? He's pretty cool. He seems different from most of these idiots.

I agreed but I didn't say anything because I was afraid you might start ignoring me if I were too enthusiastic. I didn't think about West when

I lay in my bed at night but I did think he was way cool and nice.

Then you said, Maybe you should go out with him.

When I looked at you in shock, as if you'd just told me to jump into the Tujunga Wash or something, you said, Well, he's better than Brent Fisher. If I ever have to go away or something maybe he could give you a ride to the beach.

I didn't know what you were talking about.

I do now.

S HE WANTED TO GO BACK to Phases so he took her but he was nervous as hell wondering what lovely acquaintance of Lex's they might run into. When they pulled into the parking lot they saw the Coven, as West had started calling them to himself, the girls from the funeral. Including the head witch, Justine. She saw them, too. She spat at the window of the car on Marina's side. Thick white mucus dribbled down.

Bitch! she screamed. Get the fuck out of here! What do you want?

Incest is best, one of the other girls chanted.

We're never coming back to this shithole,

West said, his tires screeching as he turned the car around.

They drove to Hollywood, to the Sunset Strip where he'd heard about a show at the Whiskey. He'd always wanted to go but he'd been scared the I.D.'s wouldn't work. Now he was pissed off enough to feel brave.

They drove under the billboards full of languishing models, past the bars and restaurants and the herds of shiny people. West could feel currents running through his blood. He wondered if he looked lit up, like Marina did, lit up from inside, her eyes flashing neon. Rodney was playing the Go-Go's. I love this song, she said, turning it up louder. West smiled, Good, 'cause that's where we're going.

It was the first time he'd seen her happy since Before, as he'd started to think of it— Before Lex Died. Maybe a little that day at the beach but this time was different. She was like a kid. She started bouncing around in her seat.

Where? The Whiskey? I don't have I.D.

West pulled two cards out of his jeans. He'd been working on them for a while, two fake driver's licenses. They were pretty good if you didn't look too close.

It turned out the bouncer hardly looked at all. It was too crowded to worry about them. The place was packed with steaming kids with shaved heads slamming around in front of the stage as if the music was hard core but of course it was only very very fast pop played by girls with short spiky hair. Marina grabbed West and pulled him into the pit, slamming her body, jumping around, bobbing her head. He wasn't afraid she'd get hurt. The boys made room or caught her and jostled her gently after she'd hurled herself into them. He wasn't afraid she'd get hurt, only that she might start to ascend into the cloud of smoke where her brother could be waiting.

Rose-in-May

I HAD A DOLL named Rose-in-May. At one point I insisted you play house with me. I wanted her to be our baby. You tolerated it for a few minutes and then you ripped off her head. I was mortified. Later, when we were older, we laughed at your brutal boyness. We laughed until we cried. Rose-in-May had been able to cry tears, too, if you poured water into her. I used salt water to make it seem more realistic.

We found Rose-in-May again, later, and decided to use her as our mailbox. She was already used to being decapitated by then, after all. We unscrewed her surprised-looking head with the stiff eyelashes and the round blue eyes that cried saltwater tears and the pursed pink rosebud mouth and we stuffed notes to each other down her ringed neck hole inside her plastic body with the little lines etched at her knees and elbows to represent dimples of baby fat.

The Rose-in-Mayl box was how I learned about your fight with Mom when she said you were spending too much time with your little sister and she wanted you to go out with some friends your own age. Rose-in-May was how you heard how grateful I was for helping me when I got my period. How I didn't like Mom's new boyfriend, Richard, because his cologne was too strong and he ignored us and his toenails made this horrible loud sound when he clipped them on the tile floor in the bathroom. Rose-in-May told me that you were quitting track because you had hurt your knee and you couldn't take the pressure, that running used to be about the way dogs run—free and joy—and now it was about winning and gritting your teeth. She told me that you were trying to write a short story, even though you were kind of scared.

Sometimes I wonder, if I found Rose-in-May and unscrewed her surprised-looking head, would there be a story in there for me?

The Note I Found

You,

I'm sorry.

I want you to know what happened.
Now maybe you can have some kind of
life.

I tried being with Michelle
Rogers but I couldn't. Maybe someday
you and Michelle will be friends again.
I know she never would have hurt you
if she knew. It was my fault. If you ever
talk to her again please tell her I said I
was sorry. But mostly I am apologizing
to you. I had to find a way to sever

myself from you and I didn't know how to do it.

I slept with this one other girl for the same reason. It didn't do what it was supposed to do. She seemed to know what was going on with us although I never told her. She said pain can give you sight or make you blind.

The reason I am telling you about these things, is so you won't hold on to an unreal memory of me. I want you to be free.

The main thing, You, is that I'm sorry.

Lex

Marina

T. S. Eliot

Quis hic locus, quae regio, quae mundi plaga?
      What seas what shores what grey rocks and
  what islands
What water lapping the bow
And scent of pine and the woodthrush singing through the
       fog
What images return
      O my daughter.

      Those who sharpen the tooth of the dog, meaning
Death
Those who glitter with the glory of the hummingbird,
  meaning
Death
Those who sit in the sty of contentment, meaning
Death
Those who suffer the ecstasy of the animals, meaning
Death

Are become unsubstantial, reduced by a wind,
A breath of pine, and the woodsong fog
By this grace dissolved in place

What is this face, less clear and clearer
The pulse in the arm, less strong and stronger—
Given or lent? More distant than stars and nearer than
    the eye

Whispers and small laughter between leaves
    and hurrying feet
Under sleep, where all the waters meet.

Bowsprit cracked with ice and paint cracked
    with heat.
I made this, I have forgotten
And remember.
The rigging weak and the canvas rotten
Between one June and another September.
Made this unknowing, half conscious, unknown, my own

The garboard strake leaks, the seams need caulking.
This form, this face, this life
Living to live in a world of time beyond me; let me
Resign my life for this life, my speech for that unspoken,
The awakened, lips parted, the hope, the new ships.

       What seas what shores what granite islands
           towards my timbers
And woodthrush calling through the fog
My daughter.

T<small>HAT</small> <small>DAY</small> <small>AT</small> <small>THE</small> <small>BEACH</small> Marina never wanted to leave the water. At one point West had to yell at her to come back. It looked like she was trying to swim away forever.

What is it? he asked, when she finally dragged herself from the surf as the dark closed in. Her hair looked black with water and she put her arms around her chest; her teeth were chattering. She ran ahead of him up the beach and started to pull on her clothes over her wet suit. Her eyes were glazed red and he realized the Santa Monica bay was a perfect cover-up for a hard cry. Between the pollution and the crash of waves. Her hands pulled at salty snarls in her hair until some hair came out.

Marina! he shouted. What is it? Then he said, softer, Hey, you. Please tell me.

He hadn't meant to use Lex's name for her—it just slipped out. And it worked. She started to cry and reached out to grasp the sleeve of his sweatshirt in her fist like a baby. She wouldn't let go. When she could talk, she said, It's so fucked up. You are going to hate me.

No I won't, he said. And he was sure of it. Not only because he knew he loved her too much for anything to make him hate her, but also because by this time he knew what she was going to say and he had already been over it in his mind and he knew he could handle it.

She just shook her head and finally he could see her lips blueing to the color of a bruise and he told her to come to the car. They sat in the parking lot over the cliffs and after a while she told him the thing he'd already guessed about her and her brother. And he didn't hate her. He didn't hate her but hearing her say it shocked him in the pit of his stomach more than he'd expected. And he was sad. Sad sad. For her and Lex and for himself. Because somehow he felt that if she trusted him enough to tell him this, yes, he was her friend, and no, she'd never think of him as anything else. Maybe, deep down, a part of West didn't even want that anymore. Maybe he felt he really couldn't handle it anymore if they made love.

But he loved her enough not to leave her, not to turn away. When she started to sob again he took her in his arms and answered every question with a whisper. Am I sick? No. It was my fault? No. Where is he? Here, here, here, West said, putting his hand gently at the hollow of her throat where he could feel her brother beating like a heart. Help me? Yes.

Nightingale

*D*ID I WOUND YOU, *mutilate. Take away your voice. Did I cut something from you. Leave you locked in silence?*

This is what you do: you sing. Every part of you. Your locks of hair sing sing, your eyes, your hands, your smile. If I listen closely I can even hear your blood.

Was I the one that took that away?

Go down to the water where we used to swim. Stand under the sky at dawn when the sky is streaked with blood. Open your mouth and shout our secret to the waves. The ocean will be your voice. You won't have to carry anything alone. Little Sister, my Spring. April. Little nightingale. Stand at the edge of the water. Your voice will come back to you. Maybe. If I am silent.

MARINA READ WEST THE T. S. Eliot poem
Lex had left inside the doll. She stopped on the
last words "My daughter." She said, Once he said
he thought he might have been my father in
another life. She stopped, scared, eyes wide, like
she realized how strange she sounded. Then she
said, He never came to the funeral. Why didn't he
come?

West said, Who, though he knew.

I'm sorry. Our dad, I mean.

Of course West had no answer to this question, except to make a suggestion.

It turned out to be easier than either of them

had ever thought, to find the dad. All they had to do was look in the mom's phone book. This was West's idea.

They went into her bedroom for the first time since he'd been coming over. The room was all red velvet and gold marbled mirrors. They looked around for the gold phone book. It was under the bed next to a pack of condoms and a vibrator.

The mysterious missing dad lived in La Jolla, the book said. There was his name, under F. John Farrell.

Marina said, Maybe I just want someone to blame, still. But he never came to the funeral. Maybe it will help.

Dad

THIS IS WHAT HAPPENED when West Minton took me to see our father. Notice how I say our father. As in yours and mine. That was when he still was.

THEY DROVE INTO THE BEACH CITY as the sun was setting, staining everything—sky, waves, sand, the white buildings along the coast—a deep red. It might have looked beautiful to West a week ago, but now it looked lurid—the color of shame. Even though there was something less toxic-looking about the sunset colors than in L.A. where the sky turned a chemical pink, and the air smelled better here. It was cooler, too. Marina had goose bumps on her arms and West made her put her jacket on.

He had told his parents the truth, mostly. There was a girl he knew, the one he'd been hanging out with, and they were going to try to look for her dad. His parents said be careful, and on his way out his dad handed him some condoms (no nudge-nudge-wink-wink; this was serious) which he figured was his good karma for not trying to steal the ones from under Marina's mom's bed (although he had to admit he had thought of it). Still, he wasn't planning to be needing any.

Marina's dad lived in one of the big houses on a cliff on the coast. It looked like a cluster of glass cylinders. West wondered if it bothered Marina that her father lived right on the ocean—the ocean she loved and felt more at home in than her own bed (even though it was a waterbed)—and she'd never had the chance to live here.

They walked up the stairs among brightly colored fake-looking flowers illuminated by hidden lights. The sun was slipping further down and darkness was welling up out of the ocean.

They could already see the moon, which was full, and West wondered if that was a good sign or not. His mom would have known. The air smelled of driftwood and beach tar and salt and full moon night.

It took awhile for someone to come to the door. They heard a man's voice merrily yell, Jan! Mike! You almost missed the best . . . He was a medium-sized, sun-crisped man with a mustache. He wasn't wearing a shirt or one of his socks and he had a lot of sandy hair on his chest. He did not seem happy to see them.

How's it going? West said.

Can I help you? No merry voice now.

Marina stepped forward into the light from the house. She had dressed up for the occasion in a pink dress from a thrift shop and pink lipstick. Her hair was washed and combed down against her head under a pink scarf. She almost looked like a housewife from the fifties, West thought. She looked beautiful but he had been getting used to her in her baggy, makeupless black.

The man seemed to become suddenly more polite when he saw her, although West thought he looked a little amused by her retro outfit. He said, Yes?

Are you John Farrell? she asked.

And you are?

Marina, she said.

It didn't register.

Farrell? Marina said.

The man's square jaw dropped and then he started laughing. Pretty good! He said, You almost had me there. He looked past them into the dark. Mike, you out there, buddy. Pretty good joke, man. Did he offer to buy you a beer in exchange for this? he asked them.

You do have a daughter, don't you? West asked, surprising himself with his own voice.

It got very quiet, just the surf whispering to the beach. The man said, You want to tell me what this is about? He was staring at Marina.

A daughter named Marina, right? You haven't seen her for a long time.

The man said, I don't know who you are, but this isn't any of your business. He was still staring. He said absently, as if to himself, She's still a kid, though.

Like about, sixteen, say? said West.

What are you trying to . . .

A woman came up behind the man. John? What's going on down here?

How's it going? Marina said to the pretty young blonde who was missing one of her shoes. I'm John's daughter, Marina Farrell. This is my friend, West Minton. We're visiting from L.A.

Oh, what a surprise! the woman said. Come in!

As they walked into the glass entry hall, she added, I'm sorry, you kind of caught us at a bad time. I hope you don't get the wrong impression.

She led them up the stairs into a round room

overlooking the water. A few other couples, missing various items of clothing, were sitting around a table drinking.

The woman introduced them and everyone stared. Then one of the men started to laugh. Just the perfect way to be reunited with your long-lost daughter, hey John! In the middle of some strip poker.

Pretty soon they were all laughing, except the dad. He said to Marina, Why don't you come in here for a minute?

West followed them and the dad gave him a look but Marina reached out and grabbed West's hand, pulling him behind her.

In the kitchen the dad had them sit on bar stools while he took another beer and the young blond woman gave them 7-Ups and salted peanuts. West's stomach was growling but he didn't want to eat and seem rude. Marina turned the sweating green can around on the counter without touching her glass.

It might have been nice if you'd called, the dad said.

Sorry, said Marina. We were just in the area.

He laughed. Oh, that makes sense. After how many—fifteen years you're in the area?

I can drive now, Marina said, as if that explained it.

I'm impressed.

Although West drove me here. But I mean I couldn't have gotten here as easily before.

I know what you mean. Listen, I'm sorry, this is just kind of a shock. You know your mother and I haven't been in touch much.

Yes. I know, Marina said. But probably recently?

The man hesitated. I was sorry to hear about that, he said.

West saw the snarl start in Marina's gentle mouth. He tried to keep breathing.

That was my brother, Lex, she said. Remember him? Your son? He died. There was a funeral.

Okay, settle down, said the dad. He gave the young woman a look that said, Leave, and she did.

I don't expect anything from you, Marina said. I never did. Neither did he. But at least you could come to his funeral!

Why don't we just calm down here, said the dad. Becky will fix you something to eat and you can sleep in the guest room. Tomorrow we can talk about it.

I don't want to eat your food or drink your drinks or watch your games, Marina said. I don't want to sleep over or talk to you tomorrow. I want to know why you didn't come to Lex's funeral. I know Mom must have called you.

We have our own lives, now, he said. It's been fifteen years.

That is such bullshit.

The man's eye twitched. He stood up. Listen, I'd have liked to talk to you rationally and explain a few things but you don't give me much choice coming in here like this. So I'll tell you straight: that was another life.

It doesn't matter. He was your son.

Actually, he wasn't, the man said. I can't believe Jackie didn't tell you? All this time?

Tell me what?

She thought she couldn't have kids.

What are you talking about?

She wanted a baby. Then you surprised us. I can see your timing hasn't gotten much better.

What are you talking about? Marina said. She turned to West. What is he talking about?

I think you better leave, the dad said. Marina's dad, but not anymore. Never Lex's dad.

The Rain Is Coming

LITTLE SISTER, *the night broke. The thunder cracked my brain finally. The rain is coming, I promise you. I didn't mean to but your tears will bring life back. Purple flowers grow, the color blood looks in the veins. They'll sprout out of my chest. I promise you they'll crack the ground, grow over the freeways, down the slopes to the sea. I'll be in their faces. I'll be in the waves, coming down on you from the sky. I'll be inside the one who holds you.*

And then I won't be.

West

THE NIGHT AFTER WE LEFT John Farrell's house we stopped at a motel by the sea and West got the key. The little yellow bungalow was humming to itself beside the little blue pool. No one seemed to be staying there but us. I don't remember much how it looked inside, except that it was small, and very clean, and the light was amber and starry, but that might have been my tears.

I called Mom first thing when we got there. She started crying and said, Why are you bringing this up now? Where are you?

I told her I had to find out. She said we'd talk when I got home. This was too much for her.

Didn't I see that?

I said I had a right to know, why didn't she tell me?

Do you think I didn't see what was between you? Do you think I could tell you he wasn't really your brother and have my children . . .

She couldn't finish it and I couldn't tell her that it had happened anyway.

I just said, Is that why you hate me?

That made her cry even more. She said, How could you think that?

I told her it seemed that he was all she ever cared about and she said, I adopted him, Marina. I wanted to have a baby and I couldn't. Do you know what that's like? Then right after he came to us I found out I was pregnant with you.

And you wished you weren't.

No. You were mine. My own child. But I was so tired. I was a mess.

You always tried to come between us.

I was trying to protect you, she said. Don't you see that?

And I knew it was true. She never wanted any of this to happen.

Come back home, Marina. Just come home.

I said I was with West Minton and we'd be back tomorrow. I expected her to yell at me but she just said to try to get some rest and drive carefully. I realized that she had given up trying to protect anyone from anything.

West. It's strange but it's only the third time I've written his name. And he's been with me almost every day. It's like somehow I'm afraid you'd be mad. But you liked West. Sometimes I think you sent him to me. I know this is crazy, but sometimes I think you might have told him about us and sent him to me.

I knew that when I told West, though, when he heard it from me, his feelings for me might change. But I had to tell him.

After a while he looked up at me and his eyes were like the lights in the pool outside the glass. He said, Isn't it harder now, that you know you could have?

I said, It's the same thing. He was my brother anyway. When someone is something to you, it's always that.

Like a friend?

You tell me.

And then we knew his feelings had changed. And changed back. And I had changed and we were new, together, about each other.

It was strange. I'd been crying nonstop for weeks since West had been with me and when we finally got into that motel room he was the one who did. He made these little heaving dry gasping sounds like an injured animal. I held him as tight as I could to try to take the pain into myself. I wish I could have done that for Lex.

But Lex wasn't there that night. The memory of him, yes, sleeping quietly in my chest. But for the first time the ghost was gone. It was just you. And me. Marina.

The Weetzie Bat Books by Francesca Lia Block:

"Transcendent." —*The New York Times Book Review*
"Tenderly intoxicating." —*Spin*
"Lyrical, resonant fables." —*The Village Voice*

Fifteen years ago Francesca Lia Block made a dazzling entrance into the literary scene with what would become one of the most talked-about books of the decade: *Weetzie Bat*. Now, the four additional Weetzie Bat Books that followed are available in two separate packages. The cherished *Witch Baby* and *Cherokee Bat and the Goat Guys* have been joined for the single volume **Goat Girls**—while their brother books, *Missing Angel Juan* and *Baby Be-Bop*, have been given a new life in **Beautiful Boys**. Rediscover the magic of all the Weetzie Bat Books, Francesca Lia Block's sophisticated, slinkster-cool love song to L.A.

GOAT GIRLS
Pb 0-06-059434-9

WEETZIE BAT
Pb 0-06-073625-9

BEAUTIFUL BOYS
Pb 0-06-059435-7

Joanna Cotler Books
An Imprint of HarperCollinsPublishers

www.francescaliablock.com